Herbster Readers

SHARING THE GREEN BALL

Written by Cecilia Minden and Joanne Meier • Illustrated by Bob Ostrom
Created by Herbie J. Thorpe

ABOUT THE AUTHORS

Cecilia Minden, PhD, is the former director of the Language and Literacy Program at the Harvard Graduate School of Education. She is now a reading consultant for school and library publications. She earned her PhD in reading education from the University of Virginia. Cecilia and her husband, Dave Cupp, live outside Chapel Hill, North Carolina. They enjoy sharing their love of reading with their grandchildren, Chelsea and Qadir.

Joanne Meier, PhD, has worked as an elementary school teacher, university professor, and researcher. She earned her BA in early childhood education from the University of South Carolina, and her MEd and PhD in education from the University of Virginia. She currently works as a literacy consultant for schools and private organizations. Joanne lives in Virginia with her husband Eric, daughters Kella and Erin, two cats, and a gerbil.

ABOUT THE ILLUSTRATOR

Bob Ostrom has been illustrating children's books for nearly twenty years. A graduate of the New England School of Art & Design at Suffolk University, Bob has worked for such companies as Disney, Nickelodeon, and Cartoon Network. He lives in North Carolina with his wife Melissa and three children, Will, Charlie, and Mae.

ABOUT THE SERIES CREATOR

Herbie J. Thorpe had long envisioned a beginning-readers' series about a fun, energetic bear with a big imagination. Herbie is a book lover and an avid supporter of libraries and the role they play in fostering the love of reading. He consults with librarians and matches them with the perfect books for their students and patrons. He lives in Louisiana with his wife Misty and their daughter Carson.

The Child's World

Published in the United States of America by The Child's World®
1980 Lookout Drive • Mankato, MN 56003-1705
800-599-READ • www.childsworld.com

Acknowledgments
The Child's World®: Mary Berendes, Publishing Director
The Design Lab: Kathleen Petelinsek, Design
Colorist: Richard Carbajal

Library of Congress Cataloging-in-Publication Data
Minden, Cecilia.
  Sharing the green ball / written by Cecilia Minden and Joanne
Meier ; illustrated by Bob Ostrom.
      p. cm. — (Herbster readers)
  Summary: "In this simple story belonging to the first level of
Herbster Readers, young Herbie seeks a replacement for the
ball he accidentally destroys"—Provided by publisher.
  ISBN 978-1-60253-006-5 (library bound : alk. paper)
  [1. Play—Fiction. 2. Bears—Fiction.] I. Meier, Joanne D.
II. Ostrom, Bob, ill. III. Title.
  PZ7.M6539Sh 2008
  [E]—dc22   2008002585

Herbie and Michael were playing ball.

The ball went up high.
It bounced off the curb.

It rolled into the street and under a car.

"Oh no," said Herbie.

"What can we do?" asked Michael.

Hank came out to play.

14

He had a green ball.

"Can we play with your ball?" asked Herbie.

"No," said Hank.

"You can play with my green racing car," said Herbie.

"No," said Hank.

"You can play with my green yo-yo," said Michael.

"No," said Hank.

"What do you want to play with?" they asked.

"You!" said Hank.

All three boys had fun
with Hank's green ball.